A Note from Mic...
Ballet Surprise

Hi! I'm Michelle Tanner. I'm nine years old. And I'm an awful ballerina!

But please don't tell anyone—at least not anyone in my family! You see, I just got a role in the school ballet. And my whole family can't wait to see me perform. But they're in for a surprise—a huge surprise!

I hope they love my ballet surprise. But it's hard to please them *all*—because I have such a huge family!

There's my dad and my two older sisters, D. J. and Stephanie. But that's not all.

My mom died when I was little. So my uncle Jesse moved in to help take care of us. So did Joey Gladstone. He's my dad's friend from college. It's almost like having three dads. But that's still not all!

First Uncle Jesse got married to Becky Donaldson. Then they had twin boys, Nicky and Alex. The twins are four years old now. And they're so cute.

That's nine people. Our dog, Comet, makes ten. Sure, it gets kind of crazy sometimes. But I wouldn't change it for anything. It's so much fun to live in a full house!

FULL HOUSE™ MICHELLE novels

The Great Pet Project
The Super-Duper Sleepover Party
My Two Best Friends
Lucky, Lucky Day
The Ghost in My Closet
Ballet Surprise
Major League Trouble
My Fourth-Grade Mess

Available from MINSTREL Books

FULL HOUSE™
Michelle

Ballet Surprise

Jean Waricha

A Parachute Press Book

A MINSTREL® BOOK

Published by POCKET BOOKS
New York   London   Toronto   Sydney   Tokyo   Singapore

A MINSTREL PAPERBACK *Original*

A Minstrel Book published by
POCKET BOOKS, a division of Simon & Schuster Inc.
1230 Avenue of the Americas, New York, NY 10020

A Parachute Press Book

READING Copyright © 1996 by Warner Bros. Television

FULL HOUSE, characters, names and all related indicia are trademarks of Warner Bros. Television © 1996.

ISBN: 0-671-53574-9

First Minstrel Books printing January 1996

10 9 8 7 6 5 4 3

A MINSTREL BOOK and colophon are registered trademarks of Simon & Schuster Inc.

Cover photo by Schultz Photography

Printed in the U.S.A.

Ballet Surprise

Chapter

1

♥ "Whoa, Comet," Michelle Tanner shouted to her dog.

It was Friday afternoon. Nine-year-old Michelle was walking Comet, the family golden retriever.

"Stop, Comet! Stop!" she cried as Comet dragged her down the sidewalk. But Comet just charged ahead—and stomped into a big mud puddle.

"Oh, no! Now look what you've done." Michelle stared down at her new white sneakers. They were covered in mud. Dirt, grass, and leaves splashed across her new pink jeans. Comet was filthy, too.

"Dad's not going to be too happy when he sees us," Michelle moaned as she and Comet walked back to the house.

Michelle opened the back door to the Tanner house. "Stay, Comet," she commanded. "You're too dirty to come inside."

"Rrufff!" the dog answered. He scooted right past her into the kitchen. He headed straight for his water dish. Then he drank and drank and drank. Water splashed all over the floor.

"Hello?" Michelle called. "Anybody home?"

Nobody answered. But she heard the sound of the vacuum cleaner start up. That must be Dad, Michelle thought.

Michelle's father, Danny, was always cleaning. He loved a very neat and spotless house.

Michelle filled up Comet's dish with

more water. "Now don't make a big mess," she said. She set the dish back down on the floor. "You know Dad doesn't like water all over the place."

"Michelle?" Stephanie called from the living room. Stephanie was Michelle's thirteen-year-old sister. Michelle could just barely hear her over the vacuum cleaner. "Is that you, Michelle? I've got something to show you."

Before Michelle could answer, Stephanie burst through the kitchen door. She held one hand behind her back, hiding something.

"Look at you!" Stephanie cried. "You're all muddy! Why are you always such a mess?"

"I'm not always such a mess," Michelle replied. She quickly brushed the leaves from her jeans.

"How are you ever going to be a star ballerina when you're covered with mud?" Stephanie asked.

"Huh?" Michelle said. She wiped a strand of her strawberry-blond hair from her face. A muddy leaf fell from the strand. "Ballerina? I'm not a ballerina— I'm a tap dancer. Remember? I take *tap* dancing lessons."

Stephanie held up what she was hiding behind her back. It was a piece of paper.

"Maybe you're not a ballerina now," Stephanie said, "but you're going to be."

Michelle glanced at the paper. There was a picture of a ballerina on it. "What are you talking about?" she asked.

"Come into the living room, and I'll explain everything," Stephanie answered.

Michelle followed Stephanie into the living room. Danny was vacuuming there. But when he saw Michelle and Stephanie, he quickly shut off the vacuum. "Michelle!" he exclaimed. "Look how dirty you are!"

"Listen to this," Stephanie interrupted him. She pointed to the piece of paper.

"They're having tryouts on Monday for the ballet."

"What ballet?" Michelle asked.

Danny glanced over Stephanie's shoulder to read. "Oh, *Nature on Parade.*"

"What's *Nature on Parade?*" Michelle asked.

Just then the front door swung open. Michelle's eighteen-year-old sister, D.J., walked in.

"Guess what, D.J.?" Danny said. "Tryouts for *Nature on Parade* are on Monday!"

"Cool!" D.J. smiled. "Hey, Steph, remember that ballet?"

"How could I forget?" Stephanie grinned. She raised her arms above her head and spun around like a ballerina. "I was the star—the Nature Fairy."

"Well, don't forget, so was I," D.J. reminded her. She started twirling around the room, too.

Michelle watched her sisters as they

jumped and twirled. Both of them were very good ballerinas. Michelle wished she were good at ballet, too. She had started taking lessons once. But she never felt graceful, so she took up tap dancing lessons instead.

"Michelle," D.J. said, plopping down on the couch, "you've just got to try out for the school ballet. It's so much fun being on stage. The scenery is wonderful. The costumes are beautiful. It's like a dream!"

"It's the best!" Stephanie piped in. "You just have to try out. And you have to get the starring role. It's up to you to keep up the Tanner tradition!"

"You'd be a great Nature Fairy, Michelle," Danny added as he walked toward the kitchen. "Just like your sisters. Now, everyone—let's get ready for dinner."

At the dinner table everyone talked about the tryouts for *Nature on Parade*. They were all so excited for Michelle.

"If you have any questions about show

business, just let me know," Joey offered. Joey was Danny's best friend. He lived in the basement apartment in the Tanner house. He and Danny hosted a morning talk show together. He was used to being onstage a lot.

Michelle's uncle Jesse wanted to help, too. "If you need any advice about your costume or hair or makeup," Jesse said, "Becky and I will help you." Becky was Jesse's wife. They lived upstairs with their four-year-old twin boys, Nicky and Alex.

"And D.J. and I can help you learn the ballet steps," Stephanie offered.

What if I don't want to be in the ballet? Michelle thought to herself as everyone around the table smiled at her. What if I don't try out?

Michelle sank down in her chair. It didn't look as if she had a choice.

Chapter 2

♥ Late the next morning Michelle still hadn't made up her mind about the ballet tryouts. She lay in bed for a whole hour thinking about what she should do.

She thought about it while she brushed her teeth. She thought about it while she got dressed. And she was thinking about it while she ate her morning cereal. She was thinking so hard that her Rice Krispies started to look like ballet slippers.

"Michelle, can you come in here?" Joey called from the living room.

Michelle put down her spoon and walked into the living room.

"Surprise!" everyone shouted. Joey, Jesse, Aunt Becky, D.J., Stephanie, and Danny were all there, standing around the living room table. On it were a couple of great big boxes.

Michelle's eyes popped wide open. "What is this?" she asked.

Joey picked up a purple box and handed it to her. "Here. Open mine first," he said.

Michelle lifted the top and peeked inside. "Wow!" she said, holding up two leotards. One was bright purple and the other was bright orange. "Thank you! Thank you!"

"Do you really like them?" Joey asked.

"I love them!" Michelle cried.

"Great!" Joey said. "Otherwise, I'd have to wear them myself. And they're really not my color."

Michelle giggled.

"Well, I'm really glad you like them,"

Joey said. "I wanted to get you something that would make you stand out onstage."

"Come on, Michelle. Open the rest," Danny said, handing her a box decorated with colored sparkles.

Michelle pulled out a pair of sparkling red ballet slippers covered with red glitter. "They're beautiful!" she exclaimed.

"They reminded me of Dorothy's shoes in *The Wizard of Oz*. I thought they were cute, just like you," Danny said and winked.

"I love them!" Michelle cried as she slipped them on. Then she twirled around in them. "They fit perfectly."

"Wow!" Stephanie gasped. "You sure don't look like a mess anymore!"

"You look just like a ballerina," Uncle Jesse said. "You're sure to get the best part."

"Why don't you try on one of your new leotards so we can get the whole picture," Aunt Becky suggested.

Michelle didn't have to be asked twice. She gathered up all the new stuff and ran upstairs. In her room she found an old pair of bright blue tights to put on with her bright orange leotard. Then she stepped into her red ballet slippers.

Before Michelle ran downstairs, she checked herself out in the mirror. Her shoes sparkled. Her leotard fit perfectly. I look just like Stephanie and D.J. when they were ballerinas, Michelle thought.

"Here I come!" she yelled from the top of the stairs. Michelle pranced down the stairs and stopped at the bottom. She raised her arms over her head—just the way Stephanie did when she practiced ballet.

"You look like—a rainbow," Jesse said.

A big smile spread across Michelle's face.

"Way to go, Michelle," Joey cheered. "And since you're dressed for the stage, I would like to take this time to show you the proper way to take a bow."

"Good idea," Danny said. "Michelle is sure to take a lot of bows after her performance."

"Oh, yes," Stephanie added. "When I performed in the school ballet, I had four curtain calls. I took four long bows."

"Well," D.J. said, "I think I had to return *five* times for bows."

"You're right, D.J.," Stephanie said. "That was the time you tripped and fell off the stage. Right after your fifth bow."

"I did not," D.J. shot back. "I don't remember that at all."

"Never mind. Never mind," Danny interrupted. "Let Uncle Joey show Michelle how to take her bows."

Joey took Michelle by the hand and led her to the middle of the room.

"This is how you do it. Watch me." Joey placed one hand behind his back and one across his stomach. Then he bent forward from the waist. "Now you try," he said to Michelle.

Michelle stepped forward. Everyone in the room began to clap—just as if she were on a real stage, and it was the end of the ballet performance.

Michelle smiled at her audience, lowered her head, and bent over from the waist. A perfect bow.

"I can't wait to try out for the school ballet!" she announced. "I can't wait!"

Chapter 3

♥ Michelle wore her new leotards all weekend. She started to think that being in the school ballet would be loads of fun. Stephanie and D.J. gave her tips on some of the steps. They even performed some of the highlights of the ballet.

By Sunday night Michelle was really excited. She could picture herself as the Nature Fairy.

Michelle decided to call her friend Mandy Metz to tell her about the tryouts. Mandy was one of Michelle's best friends from school—and a terrific ballet dancer.

She had taken ballet lessons for many years.

Michelle dialed Mandy's number. After a few rings Michelle heard her friend's voice on the other end. "Guess what?" Michelle said.

"What?" Mandy asked.

"I'm going to try out for the school ballet tomorrow!" Michelle replied.

"Me, too," Mandy said. "Hey, I didn't know you were going to try out."

"Well, I decided at the last minute," Michelle said. "You know both my sisters were in the ballet—as the Nature Fairy—"

"The Nature Fairy?" Mandy cut in. "Wow! They must be really good dancers. I really, really hope I get the part of the Nature Fairy, too," Mandy said excitedly.

Wait a minute, Michelle thought. *I'm* supposed to be the Nature Fairy! That's what the Tanner tradition is all about. I have to be the Nature Fairy—just like D.J. and Stephanie.

"So have you been practicing?" Mandy asked, interrupting Michelle's thoughts.

"Uh, yeah. A little," Michelle replied. "D.J. and Steph showed me some steps. And I learned how to bow."

"To bow?" Mandy asked.

Then Michelle heard Mandy's mom's voice. "Dinnertime."

"Well. Gotta go," Mandy said. "See you in school tomorrow."

Michelle hung up the phone. She felt terrible. Maybe I won't get the part of the Nature Fairy, she thought. But I'm a Tanner, Michelle reminded herself. And Tanner sisters were born to be Nature Fairies!

Michelle suddenly felt better. She dashed up to her room to pick out a leotard for the tryouts. Purple? Nah, everybody wears purple. Orange? That might be too bright.

Michelle couldn't decide what to wear. "I know. I'll ask Stephanie," she said aloud. "She knows a lot about ballet."

Michelle found Stephanie downstairs in the kitchen playing with Comet.

"Stephanie," Michelle began, "I can't decide which of my new leotards to wear to the tryouts. What do you think?"

"Actually," said Stephanie, "I have a wonderful idea! Come with me."

Stephanie led Michelle upstairs to the attic. Michelle watched while Stephanie opened up a very old trunk. Inside were layers of old ballet costumes that Stephanie had worn. Finally Stephanie found what she was looking for.

"Since you're going to try out for the part of the Nature Fairy, then you should look like a Nature Fairy," Stephanie said.

Stephanie held up a pink satin top and a pink lacy skirt. Two pink wings were attached to the back.

"It's the costume I wore on the night of my ballet," Stephanie explained. "Dad had it made especially for me—so I got to keep it."

Michelle took a long look at the costume. "You want me to wear *that?*"

"Why not?" Stephanie asked.

"Isn't it too fancy?" Michelle asked.

"Oh, no," Stephanie answered. "It's really important that you look your best. To be a fairy, you've got to look like a fairy!"

Michelle gazed at the costume again. It sure was pretty. Maybe Stephanie was right. Maybe wearing the costume would help her win the part.

Chapter
4

 The next day at school Michelle stared up at the clock in Mrs. Yoshida's fourth-grade classroom.

"Psst," Michelle heard her best friend, Cassie Wilkins, whisper. "Only one more minute!"

Cassie sat next to Michelle and was Michelle's other best friend—besides Mandy. Cassie was trying out for the ballet, too.

Michelle flashed her a thumbs-up.

Brrriinngg! The school bell rang. Time for tryouts!

All of the kids jumped out of their seats.

They headed straight for the cubbies to grab their backpacks. But Michelle just sat there. She was a little nervous.

"Come on, Michelle," Mandy said.

"Yeah, we're going to be late for tryouts if we don't hurry up and get dressed!" Cassie added.

Michelle followed Cassie and Mandy to the girls' locker room. Some of the other girls in her class were already there and dressed. And they were all wearing black leotards.

Michelle peeked at her two best friends. Both of them were pulling on black leotards, too.

Michelle opened her bag and stared at Stephanie's bright pink costume. She felt embarrassed. Everyone was wearing a black leotard. What am I going to do? she thought. I can't wear this.

"Why aren't you getting dressed?" Mandy asked her. "You're going to be late."

"I'll be there in a minute," Michelle said.

"Do you want me to wait?" Cassie asked.

"No," Michelle answered. "I'll be right there."

After everyone left the locker room, Michelle pulled out her costume. She had to put it on—she had nothing else to wear! It was the pink costume—or no tryouts at all!

It took Michelle a long time to change. It was hard to get the fairy wings on straight. But finally she was ready. She slipped her feet into her new red slippers and headed for the school auditorium. All the other girls were already onstage.

At first no one noticed her. Then her fairy wings started to flap back and forth. Flap, flap, flap.

Everyone turned to stare at Michelle as she tiptoed up the aisle. Flap, flap, flap. A few girls started to giggle.

Cassie ran over to Michelle. "What are

you wearing?" she asked. "What are those things on your back?"

"It's Steph's old Nature Fairy costume," answered Michelle, "Don't you like it?"

"Well, it's different," Cassie remarked.

"Cassie, I feel kind of dumb," Michelle admitted. "Everyone's looking at me."

"They're just jealous," said Cassie. That made Michelle feel a little better.

Ms. Ribas, the ballet teacher, clapped her hands to get everyone's attention.

"Please sit on the floor," she said. "I will explain how we will proceed with the tryouts."

Ms. Ribas was a ballet teacher at a local ballet school for beginners. She was very tall and thin. Michelle didn't like all the makeup she wore. But she did like the way Ms. Ribas pulled her dark hair into a bun on the top of her head. Michelle also liked the way she walked so straight.

Ms. Ribas wrote down each girl's name on a big yellow pad. Then she asked everyone to sit in the front row of empty seats. She would call each girl up onstage one at a time.

Michelle sat next to Cassie and Mandy. Mandy was called onstage first.

Ms. Ribas sat down at her piano. When she began to play, Mandy skipped smoothly across the stage. She seemed to spin, leap, and bend her arms perfectly.

Wow, thought Michelle. Mandy is really talented. She's much better than I am. She's almost as good as D.J. and Stephanie!

"She's like a real ballerina!" Cassie whispered in Michelle's ear. "She can do all the steps. Do you think she'll get the part of the Nature Fairy?"

Michelle shrugged her shoulders. She was way too nervous to say a word.

Michelle waited her turn. She watched each girl dance.

"Michelle Tanner," Ms. Ribas finally called.

Michelle wiped her sweaty palms on her pink tights. "That's me," she said, standing up.

"Come right up onstage, dear," Ms. Ribas said.

Michelle climbed the stairs to the stage. Flap, flap, flap. Her wings clapped loudly behind her.

"Oh, my!" Ms. Ribas exclaimed. "That is a very fancy costume you're wearing."

"It's my sister Stephanie's," Michelle explained. "She danced in the ballet when she was in the fourth grade."

"Oh, yes," Ms. Ribas said. "I remember that costume now! You must be Stephanie and D.J.'s little sister."

"Yes," Michelle answered quietly.

"Your sisters were such lovely ballerinas," Ms. Ribas said. "And," she added as she turned toward the rest of the girls, "they both performed the role of the Nature Fairy!"

Ms. Ribas went on and on about Stephanie and D.J. How they were two of the best ballerinas she had ever taught.

Michelle cringed. Would she be as good as Stephanie and D.J.? she wondered.

"You must be a talented ballerina, also!" Ms. Ribas exclaimed. "Now, let's see some of your turns!"

Michelle stood up on her toes as high as possible. She lifted her arms in the air—just as D.J. and Stephanie had shown her. She turned slowly. When she finished, she let out a sigh of relief.

Then she started her second turn. But her feet got all tangled up. She tripped and fell to the floor.

She pulled herself up, adjusted her tights, and tried once more. But she fell again.

"All right, Michelle," Ms. Ribas said. "Let's try something else. Do you see that cushion in the middle of the floor? Just pretend that it is a river with a crocodile in it. Run to the river and leap over it."

That sounds easy, Michelle thought. She hurried to one end of the stage. Then she ran toward the cushion. But when she reached the cushion, she skidded to a stop.

"Uh, sorry," Michelle mumbled. "I wasn't ready."

"Take your time, dear," said Ms. Ribas. "Try it again."

Michelle walked back to the end of the stage. She took a deep breath, then ran toward the cushion.

This time she leaped over it. But she landed on one foot, lost her balance, and fell over.

"Can I try it one more time?" Michelle asked.

"Whenever you're ready," Ms. Ribas said.

This time Michelle ran to the cushion, stopped, then jumped over.

TTHHUUDD! She landed hard on both feet.

Michelle threw her hands up in the air.

I did it! She glanced over at Ms. Ribas. Ms. Ribas had a strange smile on her face.

"Could you do a few twirls for us?" Ms. Ribas asked.

"Sure," Michelle said. "Twirls are my specialty."

Michelle spun around and around. She did this all the time at home—no problem. But today Michelle started getting dizzy. She found herself staggering off the stage into the wings.

"Here I am," she said, wobbling back to center stage.

"That was very, um, interesting," Ms. Ribas commented. She still wore that strange smile on her face. "Well, thank you, Michelle. I'm sure we have a special part in the ballet for you."

Michelle's heart was thumping. She wasn't really sure how well she danced. But Ms. Ribas did say that she had a "special" part for her. Could it be the Nature Fairy?

Chapter 5

♥ The next day Michelle could hardly wait to check the list to see what part she had won. Right after lunch she, Cassie, and Mandy ran off to the auditorium. A crowd of fourth graders gathered around the bulletin board, which was posted next to the auditorium door.

"There's the list," Mandy said. "Let's look."

"What if I didn't make it?" Michelle said. "Cassie, you go look and tell me. I'm too nervous."

"But I'm just as nervous," Cassie said.

"All right," said Mandy. "I'll check it."

Mandy walked over to the list and slowly read every name.

"No," she said sadly, "I don't see either of your names."

"What?" Michelle blurted.

"I'm just kidding," Mandy said. "Both your names are here. Cassie . . . you're a bluebird!"

"Cool!" Cassie cried. "I'm a bluebird!"

"And Michelle . . ." Mandy read slowly, "you're the Mountain Princess."

Michelle pushed her way through the crowd to look at the list closely. Sure enough—there was her name!

MICHELLE TANNER—MOUNTAIN PRINCESS

"Wow," Michelle said aloud, "I'm a princess!" An actual ballerina princess! she thought to herself. So what if it's not the Nature Fairy. A princess sounds much better.

"Where's your name, Mandy?" Michelle asked.

"Up there." Mandy pointed to the top of the list. "I'm the Nature Fairy." Mandy beamed.

"That's great," Michelle said. She was really happy for her. "You deserve it."

"I can't believe we all made it!" Cassie cried.

"Yeah, we'll all be together," said Michelle. "This is going to be fun."

The three girls linked arms and ran off to the cafeteria for lunch. Mandy headed straight for their favorite table to save three seats. Cassie and Michelle stood in the food line.

Cassie always ate cafeteria food. Her mother liked her to eat a hot meal for lunch. Michelle usually packed a lunch— except on Thursdays. Thursday was pizza day!

But this Thursday was like no other Thursday. Michelle was now a ballet dancer. She had to eat differently. She ordered a salad.

"You're eating a salad?" Cassie asked. "Today is pizza day. You always get pizza."

"Well," Michelle said, "Stephanie says dancers should eat light. So I'll just eat a salad for lunch."

"Oh," Cassie said.

"And maybe some french fries and chocolate pudding for dessert," Michelle added.

"That's more like it," Cassie said with a giggle.

At the lunch table Mandy took a bite out of her sandwich.

"Michelle," Mandy said, "I can't believe both your sisters were in this very same ballet."

"Yep," Michelle said. "And they were both excellent Nature Fairies."

"I hope I'm just as good," Mandy said.

"I hope you're not mad that I got the part."

"Oh, no," Michelle said. "After all, you're a really great dancer. Besides, I'm the Mountain Princess. Mountain Princess—that sounds cool, huh?"

"Totally cool," Mandy said.

"It sounds better than cool—and better than a bluebird!" Cassie joked.

Michelle smiled. She couldn't wait to tell D.J., Stephanie, and her whole family about her part. Mountain Princess—she loved the sound of it.

Chapter 6

 After school Michelle called home to tell everyone about her role. But no one answered. She left a message saying she was going to rehearsal and that Cassie's mom would drive her home.

When Michelle entered the auditorium, Ms. Ribas asked everyone to join her onstage. All the kids climbed up and sat on the floor.

Michelle listened closely while Ms. Ribas explained what the ballet was about. It was all about the different seasons of the year.

"We will start with winter," Ms. Ribas said. "All snow characters stay onstage. Everyone else will work offstage.

Michelle stood up to leave.

"Michelle," Ms. Ribas called. "You need to stay. Please, come over here with me. Your part is special."

Michelle headed over to Ms. Ribas. She felt really special. Ms. Ribas had picked *her* out for a special part!

Ms. Ribas led Michelle over to a small platform in the middle of the stage. On it stood a little chair.

"Michelle," Ms. Ribas began, "you are the Mountain Princess. The Mountain Princess sits onstage throughout the ballet. From her high position she watches the seasons pass around her."

The Mountain Princess *sits* onstage? Michelle repeated to herself. Then she asked, "Does that mean the Mountain Princess doesn't dance?"

"Well, let's put it this way," Ms. Ribas

started to explain. "The Mountain Princess doesn't dance much. She does a twirl each time the season changes. But that one twirl is very important. It is a sign for the others to start dancing."

One twirl, thought Michelle. Only one stupid twirl. This is terrible. No one will notice me. Everyone will be watching the dancers. I'll just be sitting like a dummy in the background. What will everyone in my family think?

"Now don't get me wrong," Ms. Ribas went on. "Don't be fooled. This part isn't as easy as it sounds. You have to sit very, very still throughout the entire play. And that's not easy."

Big deal, Michelle thought.

"The great part is," Ms. Ribas continued, "you get to wear four different costumes. Won't that be fun?"

"I guess so," Michelle mumbled. Then she climbed onto the platform and sat on the chair. She sat, and sat, and sat.

The snowflakes danced around her. The bluebirds twirled and swirled. The bees and flowers tiptoed around her. And now the fall leaves were fluttering across the stage.

And the whole time Michelle tried to sit very still. Ms. Ribas was right. It wasn't easy. Sometimes she just had to move. But when she squirmed, or twisted, or leaned to one side, Ms. Ribas always noticed.

Michelle couldn't help it. Like right now. She had an itch on her nose. She just had to scratch it.

And as she scratched it, Ms. Ribas called, "Sit still, Michelle."

Michelle really tried to concentrate on doing her part right. But when it was time for her to twirl, she forgot. "Pay attention, Michelle!" Ms. Ribas shouted. "Twirl!"

Michelle was so happy when Ms. Ribas finally announced that rehearsal was over. She was tired. Her back was stiff. And her bottom was sore. She limped out of the auditorium.

When she arrived home, Michelle hoped she could sneak to her room without seeing anyone. She really didn't feel like talking about her part.

How could she tell them that she was the Mountain Princess—a princess who just sits and sits? How could she tell them that she was so sore—from sitting very, very still?

But everyone was waiting for her in the living room.

"How is our star ballerina?" Danny asked.

"I'm so tired," Michelle said dramatically. "I'm stiff and sore. I may never be able to move again.

"I guess that's the life of a dancer," Joey said.

"Put those cute little toes up on the couch," Danny said. "Tell us everything."

Michelle glanced around the room. Danny and Joey stood next to her. Uncle Jesse and Becky sat on the couch. Stephanie and D.J. were curled up on the floor. The twins were staring at her.

Everybody was waiting. Waiting for Michelle to speak. Even Comet looked interested.

All eyes—all eighteen of them—were on Michelle.

Michelle flung herself on the sofa.

Uncle Jesse pulled off her shoes and massaged her feet. Aunt Becky rubbed her shoulders.

I may not be the center of attention in the ballet, Michelle thought. But I sure am at home!

"Tell us," Jesse urged Michelle. "We're dying to know!"

"I'm the Mountain Princess," Michelle announced.

Stephanie and D.J. exchanged glances. Neither said anything.

"I don't exactly remember that part," Stephanie said slowly. "What part is that?"

Michelle thought for a minute. "Well, I am onstage a lot."

"That sounds like an important part," Uncle Joey piped in.

Danny wrapped his arm around Michelle. "You have one happy dad," he said. "Three ballerinas in the same family. I knew you were a good tap dancer. But now you're a ballet dancer, too. Just like your sisters. But then, what can I say, ballet talent must run in the family."

"Yeah," Uncle Jesse teased. "What's *your* talent? Cleaning house?"

"Now, now," Danny replied, "my talent is raising three wonderful, talented daughters."

"Please," D.J. said, "I think I'm going to be sick."

Michelle thought about her part. Maybe I should tell them about how I sit on a chair through the whole play, she thought.

But then everyone would be so disappointed.

I'll tell them. But not today. I'll tell them tomorrow. Maybe.

Chapter 7

♥ The next day Michelle took her place, center stage, and waited for Ms. Ribas to begin rehearsal. She noticed Ms. Ribas out in the auditorium, talking with two girls.

Michelle looked harder.

Those weren't just any two girls. They were D.J. and Stephanie! From their seats Michelle's sisters smiled and waved at Michelle.

"Oh, no!" Michelle exclaimed. She could feel her face turning bright red. Why did her sisters have to come?

Ms. Ribas climbed onstage.

"Okay," she said. "Is everybody ready to begin?"

"Yes, Ms. Ribas," everyone answered. Everyone except Michelle.

"Let's start at the end of Scene One," Ms. Ribas instructed.

When Michelle heard that, her heart pounded. Her twirl was coming up. This was one of her big scenes. This was her chance to impress her two older sisters.

Michelle felt her knees shake. And as it got closer to her big twirl, she was trembling all over.

Finally it was time. Michelle knew her sisters were watching her every move. She took in a deep breath, stood up on her toes, threw her arms in the air, started to twirl, and . . .

Tripped and fell!

Michelle cringed. She felt like crying. She picked herself up off the dusty, wooden floor. She didn't dare look at her sisters. She could just imagine the expression on each of their faces.

"That's all right, Michelle," Ms. Ribas said. "Get ready for the next scene."

Michelle didn't even want to think about the next scene. She just wanted to run home. She wanted to lock herself in her room and never come out.

But she had to show her sisters she could dance. She just had to. So when the next scene began, Michelle knew exactly what to do.

She took her position on the platform. When the scene began, she took a deep breath and climbed down from her spot. Slowly, she leaped across the stage in large strides. She was copying some of the dance steps she'd seen on some instructional videotapes that Stephanie had.

Keep your head up and smile, Michelle reminded herself. That's what they always say on the videotapes.

Michelle smiled as she danced across the

stage again. Now everybody can see that I'm a ballet dancer! Just like D.J. and Stephanie.

Thump! Thump! Michelle knocked over two girls.

"Michelle!" she heard Ms. Ribas shout. "What on earth are you doing?"

Michelle ignored her teacher. She wasn't finished yet. She wanted to show Ms. Ribas and her sisters just one more step. Michelle tiptoed right in front of Mandy.

"Michelle, you're messing everyone up," Mandy pleaded.

Michelle stared at her friend. Then she glanced around the auditorium. The whole room had grown quiet. The music had stopped. No one was dancing. Everyone was staring at her.

"Sorry," Michelle muttered.

"Michelle," Ms. Ribas said, "you can't just change your role like that. You're confusing everyone."

"I know," Michelle said, lowering her head.

"Your part is very important," Ms. Ribas continued. "The other dancers need you to stay center stage."

Michelle felt terrible. She had made a fool of herself in front of everyone. In front of Mandy, Cassie, and the rest of the ballet dancers. And worst of all, in front of her two sisters.

"Why don't we stop now," Ms. Ribas said, ending the rehearsal. "We'll start with Scene Two tomorrow."

Michelle grabbed her bag and headed over to D.J. and Stephanie. She kept her head down the whole way. She was too scared to face them.

But when Michelle finally looked up, her sisters were busy talking with Ms. Ribas.

"Are you still taking ballet lessons?" Michelle heard Ms. Ribas ask them. "You two were so wonderful."

Michelle waited as the three talked about the ballet—and about all the good times D.J. and Stephanie had when they were in *Nature on Parade*. Ms. Ribas said she wished she could have them back.

Oh, well, Michelle thought sadly. That's the end of the Tanner tradition.

Chapter

8

♥ "You were—uh—great," Stephanie told Michelle as they were walking home.

"Yeah. Really great," D.J. added.

"No, I wasn't," Michelle replied. "I looked dumb."

"Well, maybe, you got carried away a little," Stephanie said. "But don't worry. I can help you with your twirl if you'd like."

"Okay," Michelle answered. "I guess I could use a little help. But could you do me another favor?"

"What's that?" D.J. asked.

"Please don't tell Dad about my part,"

Michelle said. "I don't want him to think I'm a lame ballerina."

D.J. and Stephanie exchanged glances and then shrugged.

"Sure, Michelle," D.J. said. "But it's no big deal. Dad won't be mad about your role."

"Please," Michelle pleaded.

D.J. and Stephanie promised to keep her role a secret. Michelle wasn't sure if that made her feel better or worse. She knew Dad would find out sooner or later.

When the girls arrived home, Stephanie popped a videotape in the VCR.

Michelle sat down on the couch. "What are you doing?" she asked.

"We're going to watch a tape of my performance," Stephanie said. "It might help you."

The tape started to play. First there was some static. Then Michelle saw her father's face on the TV screen.

"Hey, there's Dad!" Michelle exclaimed.

"Hello, is this thing on?" said Danny on the TV. "What? Oh! It's starting. Okay, let's roll."

Suddenly Danny disappeared. And the ballet started. Stephanie pointed herself out. She was easy to spot. She had on the pink costume that Michelle had worn for her tryout.

Stephanie twirled all around the stage. The audience clapped and cheered.

Michelle peered closer. She thought she had spotted the Mountain Princess. She wanted to get a better look.

Click. The ballet was cut off. Static ran across the screen again.

"Wasn't I great?" Stephanie said proudly.

"Yeah, but why was the tape cut off?" Michelle asked. "I wanted to see the Mountain Princess."

"Dad messed up on the taping," Stephanie explained. "But wasn't that a terrific scene?"

"Uh—huh," Michelle agreed. "But you

don't really notice the Mountain Princess onstage at all."

"Oh, stop," Stephanie said. "Let's work on your twirls."

Stephanie stood up straight. She lifted her chin high in the air. She put her feet together and raised her arms.

"Here she is," Stephanie announced to an imaginary audience. "The great Stephanie Tanner!"

Michelle rolled her eyes.

"Now follow me closely," Stephanie instructed as she tiptoed around in a small circle.

Michelle followed her sister.

"Very good, Michelle," Stephanie said. She sounded like a schoolteacher.

Michelle knew she didn't look quite as good as Stephanie, but she did feel as though she was getting better.

"Hey, Steph," Michelle said. "Do you think you could help me make my twirl extra special?"

"Michelle," Stephanie warned. "You tried to make your part extra special today, and it didn't work."

"That's why I'm asking *you,*" Michelle replied.

"You can't just change your role!" Stephanie said.

"But my role is so boring," Michelle grumbled.

"Well, you can't change the ballet just because you don't like it!" Stephanie explained.

"Why not?" Michelle asked.

"I don't know," Stephanie said. "You're just not allowed."

"Well, that's not a good reason," Michelle said.

Stephanie sighed. "Just be happy with your role."

"I should have stuck with tap dancing!" Michelle cried. "I should never have tried out for this stupid old ballet!"

Chapter 9

 A week of ballet rehearsals went by. Every day Michelle sat on her platform in the middle of the stage—and completed her one twirl each time the season changed.

I've got to think of something to do so that everyone will notice me, she thought. I don't care what Steph says.

Michelle thought and thought—and came up with a great idea. She couldn't wait to try it out!

Ms. Ribas called for the fall leaves to appear onstage. Slowly the fall leaf dancers fluttered onto the stage.

"Swish, swish, swish!" Michelle sang along with the music. She thought the noise sounded just like falling leaves.

Fall leaves fluttered about with their hands in the air.

"Swish! Swish! Swish!" Michelle continued.

Ms. Ribas walked around the stage. Michelle knew she was trying to figure out where the swishing noises were coming from. But then the song was over, and the fall leaves fluttered off.

Ms. Ribas returned to her seat. She called for the snowflakes to appear onstage. Michelle performed her one twirl perfectly. Then she sat down.

Eight spinning snowflakes twirled around the stage.

"Swirl, swirl, swirl!" Michelle sang out.

Again, Ms. Ribas walked onstage and listened.

"Swirl, swirl, swirl!" Michelle continued.

When the snowflakes swirled off the stage, Michelle stopped.

Then Ms. Ribas called for the spring bluebirds. But this time she didn't return to her seat. She stayed up on the stage.

Michelle performed her twirl again. Six bluebirds tiptoed up. They began their bluebird dance.

"Tweet, tweet, tweet!" Michelle chirped as they hopped around the stage. "Tweet, tweet, tweet!" she sang along with the music.

"Michelle," said Ms. Ribas, "is that you? Are you making those weird sounds?"

"Do you like them?" Michelle asked. "I just thought of it! Isn't it a wonderful idea?"

"No, Michelle, it is not a wonderful idea," said Ms. Ribas. "There are no sound effects in ballet. I'm sorry, but you will have to stop. It will only confuse everyone."

"Okay," Michelle said. "No more noises."

But then another idea popped into Michelle's head. This time she was sure that Ms. Ribas would like her new surprise.

The summer flowers entered the stage. They sat cross-legged onstage. They waited for Michelle to twirl. That was their cue to start popping up and down.

But instead of twirling, Michelle climbed down from her chair. She slid over to a flower and tapped her on the head. Then she danced in and out, between the flowers.

Tap, tap, tap, she whispered to herself as she tapped each on the head.

"Michelle," whispered one flower, "what are you doing?"

She's just confused, Michelle thought to herself. She'll catch on.

"Go away," another flower said.

Maybe the girls *don't* like my tapping, Michelle pointed out to herself. Nah, can't be. She's confused, too.

So Michelle kept dancing and tapping.

Then she heard Ms. Ribas call out, "Michelle, what are you doing?"

Uh-oh! Ms. Ribas doesn't like the tapping! Maybe by the time I'm done with the scene, she'll change her mind, Michelle thought. Tap, tap, tap, she continued humming to herself.

Some flowers sat still. Others popped up and acted as if Michelle weren't onstage. Soon everyone was bumping into everyone else. A few of the flowers fell down. One flower tripped over the other. Michelle kept dancing and tapping, jumping over the flowers who had fallen.

"Stop!" Ms. Ribas shouted from her seat. "Everyone, freeze in their position." All the dancers stopped.

"Michelle," Ms. Ribas said, "what exactly do you think you're doing?"

Double uh-oh, Michelle thought. Ms. Ribas isn't happy. "Well," Michelle said, "I—uh—wanted to surprise you."

"Yes," Ms. Ribas said. "You have surprised me!"

"And," Michelle continued, "I wanted to show you that I could do more than just stand on that platform."

"Rehearsal is over, everyone," Ms. Ribas ordered. "Michelle, we need to have a little talk."

"Oooooooohhhhh!" Michelle heard all the girls murmur.

"She's in trouble!" one girl said.

Michelle walked offstage and sat next to Ms. Ribas.

"Michelle," Ms. Ribas began, "your part is very important. Everyone in the play needs you to direct them as they perform. The dancers, and even the audience, all look to you to find out what's going to happen next. You are the one who tells us when the season is about to change. The Mountain Princess is the center of the action. There's no need for you to add sound effects or dance steps."

"It's just that no one will notice me," Michelle said.

"Everyone will notice you," Ms. Ribas explained. "You'll be sitting right in the middle of the stage. And remember, you get to change costumes four times. Everyone will be looking at you because your costume will tell everyone what season it is."

"I guess," Michelle said. But she was not convinced.

"Come with me," said Ms. Ribas. "I'll show you your costumes. Once you see them, you're going to love your part."

Michelle followed Ms. Ribas to the back of the stage. They entered a little room. Michelle saw hundreds of props. Along the back stood a long rack. On it hung all the costumes for the whole cast.

Ms. Ribas pulled four hangers off the rack. Each hanger was labeled with a different season. She showed them to Michelle.

"This one," said Ms. Ribas, "is summer." The summer costume was a yellow leotard with yellow tights. "And here are spring, fall, and winter," continued Ms. Ribas. She held each one up for Michelle to see.

Spring was a green leotard with green tights. Fall was a brown leotard with brown tights. Winter was a white leotard with white tights.

"Aren't they beautiful?" Ms. Ribas asked.

Michelle didn't think they were beautiful at all. They didn't look special. In fact, they were sort of boring.

Suddenly another great idea popped into Michelle's head.

"Ms. Ribas," Michelle said, "can I take these costumes home with me? I want to show them to my dad."

"I usually don't let the students take their costumes home until after the dress rehearsal," Ms. Ribas explained.

"Well, my dad will probably want to iron out all the wrinkles. He would never let me go onstage with my costume all wrinkly."

"How could I forget?" Ms. Ribas laughed. "I remember your father clearly. When D.J. was in this ballet, your father took home all the costumes and ironed every one of them."

"That's Dad," said Michelle. Please— oh, please—let me take the costumes home, she wished to herself.

"All right," Ms. Ribas agreed. "In your case, I'll make an exception."

"Thank you!" Michelle cried. "I'll take good care of them."

Michelle stuffed the costumes into a duffel bag. Her new idea was just great, Michelle thought. It was brilliant! And everyone is going to be so surprised. This is really going to be the best ballet ever!

Chapter

10

♥ As soon as Michelle got home, she couldn't wait to start working on her surprise.

"Hi, Michelle!" Danny said as she entered the front door.

Michelle raced right past him. "Hi, Dad!"

"Bye, Michelle!" Danny called.

Michelle quickly hopped up the stairs and rushed to her room. She unpacked the four costumes, one by one. She was planning to change each one—into something fantastic!

It was going to take a lot of work. But that wasn't going to stop her.

Michelle started with the fall costume. That was the dullest. What happens in fall? she thought. Leaves fall off the trees and change colors.

"Ah! I've got it!" Michelle cried. She searched for some construction paper in red, yellow, and orange. She drew leaves on the paper and cut them out. Then she glued them all over the brown leotard.

Michelle studied the costume. Not enough leaves, she decided. Soon every inch of the leotard was covered with cutout leaves.

Still, it needed something else. Let's see, Michelle thought, leaves fall off the tree. That's it!

Michelle collected lots of colorful, old hair ribbons from her dresser. She glued them to the arms of the leotard and then glued more leaves to the tips of the ribbons.

Michelle gazed at her costume. "Just one more thing—and then it will be perfect," she said to herself.

Michelle ran outside to the yard. Near a tree she found what she was looking for— an old bird's nest. She and Joey had found it a couple of years before when they were cleaning up the backyard. Michelle had saved it, hoping another bird would lay eggs in it again. But it remained empty the whole time. Now the nest would come in handy.

Back upstairs in her room Michelle tried on her masterpiece. She slipped on the leotard, careful not to lose any leaves or ribbons.

To complete the outfit, she placed the bird's nest on top of her head. It fit just right.

Michelle was so pleased with how her costume looked, she just had to tell someone. She called Cassie and asked her to come over—right away!

Michelle took off the bird's nest. She slipped her bathrobe on over her costume. Then she went downstairs to wait for Cassie. Uncle Jesse was in the kitchen eating a snack with the twins.

"What's up?" he asked Michelle. "Why are you wearing a bathrobe in the middle of the afternoon? Are you sick or something?"

"Well, umm," Michelle said, "I'm going to take a bath later—so I thought I should get ready."

"But it's only four o'clock in the afternoon. Isn't that a little early for a bath?" Uncle Jesse asked.

"Um. You're right," Michelle admitted. But before Uncle Jesse could say anything else, Michelle heard a knock on the back door.

"Come in, Cassie!" she yelled.

"Hi!" Cassie said, following Michelle out of the kitchen. "Why are you wearing a bathrobe?"

"You'll see," Michelle answered. "Let's go upstairs."

Michelle led Cassie up to her bedroom. Then she threw off her robe—and revealed her homemade costume.

"Don't say anything yet," Michelle said. "I'm not finished." Then she plopped the bird's nest on top of her head.

Cassie stared at Michelle in amazement. "What did you do?"

"I made myself a new costume," Michelle explained. "I'm supposed to be fall. Don't you think this looks like fall with all the leaves?"

Cassie walked around Michelle.

"It looks great," Cassie said. "I love it. But . . . did Ms. Ribas say you could change the costume?"

"Well, not exactly," Michelle said

"What does that mean—not exactly?" Cassie asked.

"Ms. Ribas doesn't know yet," Michelle explained. "I thought I would surprise her.

The old costumes were so blah. This one is much cooler. She'll love it. Don't you think?"

"I don't know," Cassie said. "Let's ask Stephanie what she thinks."

"No way," Michelle said. "I don't want anyone to know about my surprise—not Stephanie or D.J. or even Mandy. Promise to keep it a secret?"

"Okay," Cassie said slowly. "If that's what you want."

"Good!" Michelle replied. "Now you have to help me do the other costumes."

Michelle showed Cassie the other plain leotards.

"How should we change this boring old white one?" Michelle asked. "I want it to really sparkle."

"I've got it," Cassie burst out. "Let's put glitter on it!"

"Great!" Michelle exclaimed. "And how about gluing on white cotton balls to look like snowflakes?" Michelle said, excitedly.

"Cool!" Cassie replied. "Let's put the cotton balls on first—then the glitter."

Michelle and Cassie went right to work. Soon every inch of the leotard was covered with cotton balls. It looked like one big cotton ball.

For the finishing touch, they sprinkled green, silver, and gold glitter all over it.

Michelle tried it on once the glue had dried.

"Wow!" Cassie cried. "That is really beautiful. There's no way anyone could miss you onstage."

Michelle gazed at herself in the mirror. She had to admit it—the costume looked incredible.

"Let's start another one," Cassie urged.

The two girls began working on the spring costume.

Then suddenly Michelle heard someone

yelling from downstairs. "D.J. I'll help you out later on. I'm just going up to change!"

It was Stephanie—and she was on her way up to their room!

"Oh, no!" Michelle cried. "Stephanie's coming! We have to hide everything!"

"Where?" Cassie asked.

"Just shove everything under the bed," Michelle answered. "I'll run downstairs and try to stall her."

Michelle charged out of her bedroom and shut the door behind her. She met Stephanie in the middle of the staircase. "Hi, Steph," she said, blocking the way. "How's school? What's new? How's it going?"

"What's wrong with you?" Stephanie asked.

"Nothing. I'm just excited . . . I'm excited about the school ballet. It's only two days away." Michelle plopped down on the steps in front of Stephanie.

"Well, I'm glad you're excited," Stephanie replied. "But move out of my way. I want to change out of my school clothes."

"Why?" Michelle shrieked. "You look terrific! You should wear your school clothes all day."

"Michelle, move out of my way," Stephanie said. "Unless there's some reason why you don't want me to see the bedroom."

"Of course not," Michelle answered quickly. "How could you even think of such a thing? Why don't we go to the kitchen and discuss this distrust of me?"

"Good try, Michelle," Stephanie said, stepping past her. "Sure there's nothing you want to tell me?" she asked when she reached the top of the stairs.

"Nothing," Michelle mumbled. She followed Stephanie to their room. At the door Michelle slipped in front of her sister and placed her hand on the doorknob.

"We're coming into the room!" Michelle shouted loudly.

"Out of my way, Michelle," Stephanie grumbled.

"Okay, here we come!" Michelle shouted every word as loudly as she could. Then she slowly opened the door. She closed her eyes—she couldn't look.

"Hi, Cassie," Stephanie said. "Have you noticed how crazy Michelle is acting?"

"Not really," Cassie replied.

Michelle opened one eye and peeked around the room. Everything was hidden! Michelle's secret would be safe—until the night of the ballet!

Chapter 11

♥ Finally it was Friday. The day of the dress rehearsal for *Nature on Parade*. And only one day till the ballet!

Michelle sat in her seat in Mrs. Yoshida's class and stared out the window. She thought about the ballet.

Rehearsals had been fun the past few days. Michelle hadn't worried about her part. All she had thought about were her new costumes. She finished working on them the night before. Michelle thought they were amazing.

But now Michelle had a new problem.

Today was dress rehearsal. Everyone was supposed to wear their costumes. Michelle left her costumes home. She couldn't wear them yet. They were supposed to be a surprise for the ballet!

Michelle was nervous. She knew Ms. Ribas would be angry. Michelle thought about not going to rehearsal at all. She could pretend to be sick. But then Ms. Ribas would probably call her at home. Michelle decided she would just have to face her teacher.

When Michelle arrived at the auditorium that afternoon, everyone was already onstage—in costume.

"Hey, Michelle," Mandy whispered. "Where's your costume?"

"I forgot it," Michelle replied.

"But—" Mandy started.

"Places everyone," Ms. Ribas interrupted. "Places!"

The dancers lined up backstage in order of their appearance. First came the winter snowflakes, then the spring bluebirds, the summer flowers, and the fall leaves.

Michelle tried hiding behind two girls so Ms. Ribas wouldn't spot her. She was so nervous, her arms and legs began to shake.

Maybe she won't notice, Michelle hoped.

Ms. Ribas clapped her hands. "Okay, quiet everyone. We are going to run through the whole ballet, from start to finish—exactly as if this were the night of the ballet."

Everyone remained very quiet and very serious.

"Michelle," called Ms. Ribas, "please come onstage and take your position. We're ready to start!"

Michelle slowly walked onstage. She was dressed in her bright orange leotard—the one Joey had given her—and her red slippers.

"Why aren't you wearing the proper costume?" Ms. Ribas asked firmly.

"I forgot them all," Michelle replied quietly.

"Michelle, you knew today was our dress rehearsal." Ms. Ribas sounded upset.

Michelle felt awful. But she couldn't tell Ms. Ribas the truth. She didn't want to ruin her surprise.

"I'm sorry, Ms. Ribas," Michelle said. She paused, then added, "My dad washed and ironed each one of my leotards. And I didn't want to get them wrinkled or anything."

"Well, there's nothing we can do now," Ms. Ribas said. "It's too late to send you home for them. Let's get on with rehearsal!"

So dress rehearsal started. Mandy performed her solo dance. She was great. All the flowers, snowflakes, fall leaves, and bluebirds danced wonderfully, too. And Michelle sat on her platform very still— and twirled her twirls perfectly.

"Now, Michelle," Ms. Ribas said when

dress rehearsal was over, "don't forget your costumes tomorrow."

"Don't worry," Michelle answered. "I won't."

She *definitely* would remember to bring them tomorrow. Tomorrow was the big night. The night of her big ballet surprise!

Chapter
12

♥ All day Saturday Michelle was very nervous. Tonight was the night of the ballet. And now it was almost time to head over to school.

All four costumes lay spread out on Michelle's bed. Soon everyone would see them.

Michelle packed each costume carefully into a bag.

"Come on, Michelle!" Danny yelled from downstairs. "We're all ready to go. We're just waiting for you."

Michelle took a big gulp.

She picked up her bag and headed downstairs. Everyone was dressed and ready to go.

"It's okay if you're nervous," Stephanie assured Michelle. "Everyone is a little nervous."

"That's right," her dad encouraged her. "You just dance your best. I know you'll be great. After all, you're a Tanner!"

"Thanks, Dad," Michelle muttered.

Stephanie, D.J., and Michelle climbed into the backseat of the family car. Joey hopped in the front seat next to Danny. Jesse, Becky, and the twins drove in a separate car.

"Everyone comfortable?" Danny asked, fixing his tie in the rearview mirror. "This is so exciting!" he said cheerfully. "My little Michelle's big debut in the ballet!"

He started the car and backed out of the driveway. Suddenly he slammed on the brakes.

"Wait a minute!" Danny said, opening the car door. "I forgot the video camera!"

"Dad, do you have to tape the ballet?" Michelle called.

"Of course!" Joey answered for him.

"Yeah," D.J. butted in. "It's a Tanner tradition. Then later we can all watch the tape and make fun of you."

"Stop scaring your sister," Joey said, turning to the backseat. "Don't worry, Michelle. No one's going to make fun of you."

But no one knew about her costumes, Michelle thought. What will everyone think? What if they think my costumes are stupid? What if I've made a big mistake?

When they arrived at school, Michelle crawled over D.J. and jumped out of the car. She sped off to the auditorium without saying a word.

"Good luck, Michelle!" Danny called out after her.

"Remember everything I taught you!" Joey shouted.

Michelle joined the rest of the cast backstage. Everyone was running around. There were the dancers. And there were a few parents who were helping out backstage. Costumes and hairbrushes seemed to fly through the air as everyone hurried to get ready.

Michelle had to rush, too. She found a quiet corner where no one would see her. She put on her first outfit—the fall costume. She slipped the leotard on carefully. She didn't want to lose any leaves or glitter. When she was finished, she placed the bird's nest on her head. At last she was ready!

The performance was about to begin. Ms. Ribas took her place at the edge of the stage. She stood behind a wooden stand with a microphone.

A hush fell over the audience. The lights were dimmed. Michelle stood in the wings.

She waited for Ms. Ribas to signal her to take her place onstage—three taps on the wooden stand.

Tap, tap, tap. There it was.

Michelle walked onstage, climbed up the platform, and sat down. She could hear all the girls backstage whispering. Michelle knew they were talking about her. But were they laughing at her?

Just then the curtain began to rise. Sitting high in her chair, Michelle watched the curtain lift. She felt the warmth of the spotlight shining brightly on her. She hoped her costume really sparkled!

A loud gasp rose from the audience. Then the entire room grew completely quiet.

Michelle glanced over at her teacher. Ms. Ribas's face turned white. Her mouth dropped open. Her eyes looked as if they were about to pop out of her head.

Then something unexpected happened.

There was a faint sound coming from the audience—the sound of applause.

Michelle peered into the audience. She squinted her eyes. Finally she spotted her family. And discovered who was clapping—the twins!

Then her entire family began to clap. More people joined in the applause. Soon the entire audience was clapping and whistling.

Michelle's costume was a big hit!

And then the ballet began! The fall leaves danced onstage. They fluttered round and round.

As soon as the scene was over, the curtain dropped. Michelle hurried offstage for her costume change. It was time for winter.

She carefully pulled on her new costume. Then she added the final touches. She pinned white cotton puffs in her hair. And after a quick glance in the mirror, she was ready.

Michelle rushed back to her platform seat. The curtain was about to rise. She sat still and waited nervously for the audience's reaction.

The curtain finally rose. The audience grew silent once again. Then they broke out into laughter.

Oh, no. They hate it, Michelle thought. She was about to burst into tears. But suddenly the sound of laughter turned into clapping—clapping much louder than before!

They like it! Michelle breathed a great big sigh of relief.

The next scene was just as wonderful. Everybody loved her spring costume.

On her head she wore a hat that she had shaped and painted to look like a cloud. Large blue raindrops, made from shiny foil paper, hung from the bottom of the hat. A bright yellow sun was pasted on her stomach. It was made from paper, too, and was covered with gold glitter.

Two huge red tulips made out of paper grew out of her red ballet slippers. They reached all the way up to her knees. And on her arms she wore two silver metal lightning bolts. She waved her lightning-bolt arms back and forth throughout the whole scene.

Michelle couldn't wait for the last act. The summer costume was her absolute favorite.

As the curtain rose, Michelle straightened her summer costume. It was a huge sun. It surrounded her entire face. With long spikes of sunrays sticking out all over. Michelle smiled wide. On her body, a bright red line ran right down the middle. And at her shoulders the number 90° sparkled in bright red. Michelle was a thermometer!

As a finishing touch, Michelle wore large sunglasses. In her hand, she held a huge, glittery fan. She fanned herself through the entire scene.

The audience went wild. Even Ms. Ribas applauded. Michelle felt so happy. Really, really happy!

At the end of the play the best thing happened. After all the girls had taken their bows, Ms. Ribas waved to Michelle to take a bow—all by herself.

When the curtain dropped, Michelle ran off the stage—and bumped right into Ms. Ribas. But she didn't look too happy. Michelle didn't like the scowl on her face at all.

"Michelle," Ms. Ribas said sternly. "Could I please have a word with you?"

Uh-oh, Michelle thought. I'm in big trouble.

Chapter
13

♥ Michelle slowly followed Ms. Ribas over to one side.

"Michelle," Ms. Ribas started. "Your costumes were very creative. But I was very upset that you changed them without asking me first."

"I wanted to surprise you," Michelle explained.

"Next time," Ms. Ribas said, "you need to discuss this with me ahead of time."

"But I was afraid if I told you, you wouldn't let me change them," Michelle explained. "And then I would have been stuck with those plain old leotards."

"There's one thing you must understand about being in a ballet or any group performance," Ms. Ribas said. "It's all about being a part of a team. Michelle, you were so worried about yourself that you forgot about the rest of your team."

"I'm sorry, Ms. Ribas," Michelle said softly. Michelle couldn't believe it, but Ms. Ribas was right—not once did she think of anyone else in the ballet but herself.

Just then Danny joined them. "What a wonderful production," he said to Ms. Ribas. "What a success for you!"

"Thank you very much, Mr. Tanner," Ms. Ribas said.

"She was great—wasn't she?" Danny continued. "But as you know, ballet runs in the Tanner blood."

"I think it has to do more with creativity," Ms. Ribas said. "She's very talented with costume design."

"You liked my costumes?" Michelle cried happily. "I thought you hated them!"

"Yes, I liked your costumes," Ms. Ribas responded. "But that's not really the point here."

"I'm a little confused," Danny said. "Michelle, didn't Ms. Ribas know what you were going to wear?"

"Well, um, not exactly," Michelle answered. "I changed them at the—uh—last minute."

"It seems as though Michelle was bored with the ballet," Ms. Ribas explained. "So she decided to make it more interesting— by redesigning the costumes."

"But, why?" Danny asked.

"Because no one would have noticed me," Michelle said.

Danny put his arm around her. "I would have noticed you," he said.

"But my part was so small," Michelle said.

"You know, it takes big parts and small parts to put together a ballet," Danny said. "Each part is very important—no matter the size."

"I guess you're right," Michelle said. Then she added in a whisper, "Dad, I'm really not that good at ballet."

"What do you mean?" Danny cried. "I thought you were great," he replied, giving her a great big hug. "Did you hear how excited the audience was?"

"That's because of the costumes," Michelle said, "I'm not as good a dancer as D.J. and Stephanie."

"Did you think I expected you to be?" Danny asked.

"Well, sort of," Michelle started to explain. "I tried out only because I thought you wanted me to be like them."

"I don't want you to be like your sisters," Danny replied. "I want you to be yourself."

"So it's okay for me not to like ballet?" Michelle asked.

"Of course," Danny said. "I didn't even know you hated ballet."

"Nobody asked me," Michelle said.

"You're right, sweetie," Danny agreed. "I guess I did push you a little. I just got caught up with all the excitement!"

Just then Steph and D.J. came running over to them.

"Michelle!" D.J. said. "You're missing your cast party."

"Yeah," Stephanie piped in. "And you're the star!"

Michelle liked hearing those words from her sisters.

"You were the best Mountain Princess ever!" D.J. said.

"And one of the best three daughters in the world!" Danny added.

"Thanks, everybody," Michelle said with a big smile.

"Now let's have some cake to celebrate," Danny suggested as they joined the others at the party. "Then we'll go home and watch the videotape!"

※-※-※-※-※-※-※-※-※

For information about
Mary-Kate + Ashley's Fun Club™,
the Olsen Twins' only
official fan club, write to:

Mary-Kate + Ashley's Fun Club™
859 Hollywood Way, Suite 412
Burbank, California 91505

※-※-※-※-※-※-※-※-※